First edition published in 2020 by Flying Eye Books,
an imprint of Nobrow Ltd. 27 Westgate Street, London E8 3RL.

Written by Stephen Davies and illustrated by Victoria Evans,
based on the characters and storylines
created by Luke Pearson and Silvergate Media company.

HILDA™ © 2020 Hilda Productions Limited,
a Silvergate Media company

3 5 7 9 10 8 6 4 2

Published in the US by Nobrow (US) Inc.

Printed in Great Britain on FSC® certified paper.

ISBN: 978-1-912497-10-2

www.flyingeyebooks.com

Based on the Hildafolk series of graphic novels by Luke Pearson

HiLDA
AND THE
TIME WORM

Written by Stephen Davies   Illustrated by Victoria Evans

FLYING EYE BOOKS
London | Los Angeles

CONTENTS

1

Wind blew. Woffs flew. Deep, crisp snow lay all around. At the Sparrow Scout stall in Trolberg marketplace, a little girl with blue hair leaned over a steaming cauldron.

Hilda was deep in concentration on her cookery. Her wooden spoon delved into the corners of the pot, swirling and churning its invisible depths: onion and mushroom, potato and carrot, mountain garlic and fresh kintoki ginger.

The Sparrow Scout soup stall needed real teamwork. Hilda was on stirring duty, David was on chopping duty, Twig was on tail-chasing duty and Frida was on recipe management. It was her great-great-grandmother's secret recipe and Frida was determined that it be followed to the letter.

"Hurry up, everyone," said Frida. "The customers will be arriving soon."

"Yes, chop-chop, David," said Hilda.

To the left of the stall stood the Sonstansil tree, its branches heavy with large, white buds. In a land full of unusual trees, this tree was even more unusual than most. At school that morning, Hilda had researched it and had written some amazing facts in her topic book.

1. The buds of the Sonstansil tree appear on the first day of the Winter Festival.

2. They open gradually during the three nights of the festival.

3. When the last bud opens, the flowers begin to glow in the dark, an event known in Trolberg as the Big Glow.

4. The morning after the Big Glow, everybody throws parties and gives presents.

Hilda had never seen the Big Glow before, and she was very excited.

"Hey, Witch Girl," said a mean voice nearby. "Is it true that you caused last week's snowstorm? I heard that you rode a broomstick into the heart of a snowstorm and that you convinced a weather spirit to make it snow on Trolberg more than it has ever snowed before."

Trevor, the class bully, was standing on a mound of snow to the right of the Sparrow Scouts' stall.

Hilda put down her wooden spoon and scowled at him. "It wasn't a broomstick, Trevor, it was a thunderbird. And it wasn't one weather spirit, it was a whole crowd of them. And I didn't start the snow, I stopped it."

"All right." Trevor picked up a handful of snow and packed it tight between his hands. "You can stop snow, can you? Maybe we should put that to the test!"

"Go away, Trevor," stammered David.

"Bug Boy!" said Trevor. "I didn't see you there. Look everyone, Bug Boy's crying!"

"I'm not crying," said David. "I've been chopping onions!"

Kelly and Anders, two of Trevor's naughtiest friends, appeared beside him. They too were holding snowballs.

"Careful," said Frida. "The soup is boiling hot."

"Boiling hot?" Trevor grinned. "Don't worry, we'll cool it down for you."

A volley of snowballs sailed through the air. Hilda, David and Frida dived for cover under the table. Soup splashed. Peppers rolled. Their SPARROW SCOUTS banner slumped to the ground. Twig's fluffy tail puffed up to twice its normal size.

"Come out, come out, wherever you are!" came Kelly's singsong voice.

"They're seriously appreciating the cosiness under that table!" giggled Anders.

"David, Frida, listen to me," Hilda hissed. "On the count of three, we jump up, grab a vegetable – a squashy, rotten one, if possible – and we throw it at those meanies as hard as we can."

"Really?" David sounded unsure. "I thought

that hiding under here was working out pretty well so far."

"We can't let them bully us," said Hilda. "So, on the count of three. One..." She wrapped her scarf around the lower half of her face. "Two..." She crouched on the balls of her feet. "THREE!"

With a ferocious battle cry, the three friends leaped up. Hilda grabbed a tomato. Frida grabbed a potato. David, his eyes tight shut, grabbed a mushroom. They lifted their vegetables, ready to strike.

Trevor and his gang were nowhere to be seen. Instead, a broad-shouldered man and a young woman were standing in front of the stall. Both of them wore the caped brown and yellow uniforms of the Trolberg Safety Patrol.

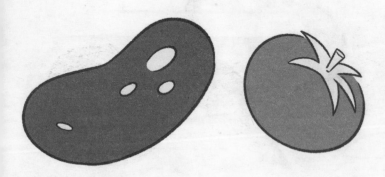

A button mushroom pinged off the big man's nose.

"David, open your eyes," hissed Frida. "You just hit a Safety Patrol officer on the nose with a mushroom."

"It's fine," said the big man, though the expression on his face said it wasn't fine at all. "Now, which of you two girls is Hilda?"

"I am," said Hilda.

"Allow me to introduce myself. I am Erik Ahlberg, commander of Trolberg Safety Patrol. This is Gerda Gustav, my deputy."

Hilda gulped. "Have I... done something?"

"Yes, you have," said Ahlberg, twirling his thin moustache. "You have won our very first ASPECT!"

Gerda let off a party popper, making David jump.

Hilda stared at the officers through tumbling confetti. "First what?"

"ASPECT," said Gerda. "Annual Safety Patrol Essay Contest Trophy."

Frida squealed, making David jump again. "The essay contest!" she cried. "Don't you remember, Hilda, in class last week Miss Hallgrim made us all write an essay on the topic 'Trolls: Perils and Preparedness'. It sounds like your essay won!"

Hilda did remember. She had written her essay about something that happened to her in the wilderness before she and Mum moved to Trolberg. She had lost track of time while sketching a troll rock and ended up having to run away from a very angry troll with a bell on its nose. As it turned out, she need not have worried. All the troll wanted was to get rid of the bell and return her sketchbook.

"You'll receive your trophy at a ceremony tomorrow morning," Ahlberg continued.

"After that, you join us on an inspection of the city's troll defences."

"I can't," said Hilda. "Tomorrow is a school day."

"Principal Magnusson has already given permission," smiled Gerda. "Commander Ahlberg will lead a special school assembly, then we'll take off from the playground in a zeppelin."

"What's a zeppelin?"

"A dirigible," said Gerda.

"What's a dirigible?"

"An airship," said Gerda. "The perfect vehicle for an adventurer."

Hilda's heart leapt. "Count me in," she said.

The dirigible was indeed a magnificent vehicle. Moored to a flagpole in the playground, it hovered low over the Edmund Ahlberg School like an immense, brooding spaceship.

Hilda stood next to Erik Ahlberg on a moveable staircase, looking out over a sea of upturned faces. Frida and David stood in the front row, grinning like loons.

"Good morning, everybody," said Erik Ahlberg in a nasal, lilting voice. "My name is Head Officer Ahlberg, the great-great-great-great-great-great-

great-great-great-great-grandson of valiant troll-slayer Edmund Ahlberg, after whom this school is named."

He paused for effect and received a smattering of applause. The loudest clapping came from inside Hilda's ear, where her elf friend Alfur sat perched. He had insisted on coming along today to research one of his "Letter from Trolberg" reports for the elves of the Northern Counties.

"Children of Trolberg!" Ahlberg cried, and the feather in his hat waggled in the breeze. "How often do you have nightmares about trolls? How often do you dream that a troll is climbing through your window to rip you from your bed and chomp you into bits? Well, here I stand with one of your fellow students, a girl who has felt actual troll breath on her cheek. In her winning essay, she described a bloodthirsty troll that lay in wait for her behind a bludbok tree—"

Hilda tugged his sleeve. "It wasn't bloodthirsty. It just wanted—"

"The troll sprang out in front of her and grabbed her round the waist with a vice-like grip"

"I didn't say vice-like."

" – lifted her to its slavering maw – "

"I didn't say slavering."

" – and roared, 'I'M GOING TO EAT YOU,
LITTLE GIRL!'"

Hilda was starting to wonder whether
Ahlberg had even read her essay. She tried to
explain about the bell and the sketchbook but her
voice was drowned out by the rantings of Head
Officer Ahlberg.

"What did our pint-sized hero do, I hear you
ask? I'll tell you what she did. She bopped him
smartly on the nose, then wriggled free and lived
to tell the tale. Good work, my girl!"

The school children clapped and stamped
as Erik Ahlberg shoved a silver trophy into
Hilda's arms.

"Such horrors must never happen again!"
Ahlberg boomed. "A new era of safety begins
today. It starts with the ringing of a single bell,
and then another and another, until this whole
great city reverberates with the bing-bong sound
of triumph!"

Ahlberg began to swing a large, cracked hand bell. Members of the school hand bell choir grabbed their own bells and joined in as best they could.

"Down with trolls!" Erik Ahlberg yelled.

"Down with trolls!" chorused the children.

"Up with us!"

"Up with us!"

Even the big school bell was clanging now. Hilda winced and stuck her fingers in her ears.

"Oi!" cried Alfur. "You're crushing me!"

"Sorry," said Hilda. "They're just so loud!"

"What do you think of the ceremony?" asked Alfur. "Thrilling, isn't it?"

Hilda did not think the ceremony was thrilling. She thought it was horrid – all that Down with trolls, and Up with us, and dinging and donging and shaking of fists.

Erik Ahlberg brought the cacophony to an end by throwing his hand bell into the crowd as a souvenir for some lucky Trolberg child. He flung it harder than he intended and a yelp of pain went up from the middle of the throng.

"And now, farewell!" Ahlberg beamed. "Up into the heavens we go, to inspect our city's troll defences!"

Hilda stepped into the airship and planted her feet wide to steady herself as it rose into the air. Pressing her nose to a window, she could see her schoolmates waving and Miss Hallgrim hopping to and fro on one foot in pain.

"So?" Ahlberg turned to Hilda expectantly. "How was I?"

"Loud," said Hilda.

Ahlberg grinned as if he had received a compliment.

"And your hand bell hit my teacher on the foot," Hilda added.

"Oops." Ahlberg grinned even more widely. "And what do you think of my airship?"

Hilda looked around at the plump leather seats, thick carpets and sparkling windows. "Very smart," she admitted.

"I call this part the Infinity Lounge," said Ahlberg. "And over there" – he gestured to the front of the ship – "is the cockpit."

Gerda Gustav sat at the controls wearing a dark blue pilot's uniform. "Hi, Hilda," she said. "Good to have you with us."

As the airship gained height, the playground shrank to the size of a postage stamp and Hilda saw the city of Trolberg spread out beneath her – silent, beautiful and blanketed in white. A flock of yellow woffs appeared alongside the airship. Hilda waved at them.

The airship drifted over the Bottle Opener bell tower and Flimflåm Bank. The scribbling noises in Hilda's ear told her that Alfur was busy taking notes.

"Approaching the Gorrill Gardens bell tower," Gerda announced.

As Hilda peered down at the bell tower, she saw that the belfry was swarming with people in hard hats. "What are those construction workers doing?" she asked.

"Installing a new bell and a mechanical bell-ringer," Ahlberg answered. "I told them to test it during our inspection, so any second now we can expect to hear a–"

BONG!!!

The airship shuddered, Hilda staggered and the flock of woffs dropped right out of the sky.

3

Even Erik Ahlberg looked shaken by the volume of the new bell. His eyes bulged and the ends of his thin moustache quivered. As the last echoes of the almighty bong resounded from Mount Halldór and Mount Hár, Ahlberg gripped the back of Gerda's chair so tight his knuckles whitened.

"WOWEE!" he yelled. "That was PROPERLY LOUD!"

"I can't hear a thing," Alfur whimpered in Hilda's ear. "That bell has frazzled my eardrums. It has discombobulated my brain. Scrambled my grammar also it has."

Hilda turned to Erik Ahlberg, while trying to soothe the elf squeaking in her ear. "What on earth was that?"

Ahlberg smiled widely, revealing a gold tooth that Hilda had never noticed before. "That was the sound of the future." he whispered.

"You mean, it's going to happen again?"

"Yes, indeed. And again and again and again and again, every fifteen minutes, day and night, until the trolls get the message."

"What message?"

"That this city isn't big enough for them and us."

Hilda stared at him. "But there aren't any trolls in Trolberg."

"I know that." Ahlberg spoke slowly and clearly, as if to a baby. "But they're close to Trolberg, Hilda, and getting closer every year. Watching and waiting. Waiting and hating. Pitching their camps a stone's throw from our walls, lighting their foul-smelling fires and plotting all kinds of evil in their mysterious languages. I've seen them, Hilda. Seen them and heard them and fled from them. And if you think I'm going to let them strike the first blow against us, you're wrong."

Anger rose in Hilda's chest. "So you're going to use insanely loud bells to drive the trolls away?"

"Precisely." Ahlberg folded his arms. "The new bell system will be put into action at a special ceremony tomorrow morning and all the pesky trolls outside our walls will be compelled to trudge right back to Troll Land, or wherever they came from."

"This is Troll Land!" cried Hilda. "They come from right here! Why do you think it's called Trolberg?"

"I mean, wherever the trolls came from originally." Ahlberg's voice was frosty. "Now listen here, Hilda. Coming with us in the Safety Patrol airship is a very great honour and we would never have selected your essay for the prize if we had known you were going to be this much trouble."

"Not half as much trouble as an angry troll!" Hilda shot back. "Your new bell system isn't going to drive the trolls away, Mr Ahlberg. It's going to rile them up. Do you want to go down in history as the man who started an actual war between trolls and humans?"

Ahlberg clenched his massive jaw and gazed across the rooftops to the mountain peaks beyond. "I don't mind if I do," he said, "and better still, as the man who won that war."

Hilda stared at him, completely lost for words.

"Oh, look," said Gerda, breaking the silence

with fake cheeriness. "The sun's come out."

Hilda stormed into the Infinity Lounge and slumped down on a leather seat. Her worst suspicions about Erik Ahlberg had been confirmed. He was clearly as aggressive and deluded as his great-great-great-great-great-great-great-great-great-great grandfather.

"That went well," muttered Alfur, whose hearing had returned.

Hilda felt close to tears. She hated getting into

arguments. But more than that, she hated cruelty to any sort of creature. Even trolls had a right to live in peace.

The floor of the Infinity Lounge was made of transparent panels. From her seat, Hilda watched the northern quarter of Trolberg slide away beneath her.

"Strange," she said out loud.

"What is?" said Alfur.

"Down there, between the ruined windmill and the Bronstad Lane footbridge, I can see a little farmhouse with a steep, sloping roof."

"So what?"

"I've never seen it before."

"Me neither," said Alfur. "But travelling in your left ear does tend to limit my view."

Hilda stared down at the snow-covered roof of the farmhouse. She had crossed the Bronstad Lane footbridge on her way to school and had not noticed this house. It must have sprung up in the last hour or so – but that was impossible!

"A reporter should have unrestricted vision," said Alfur. "Perhaps I could travel under your

beret, with some kind of periscope poking out the top. That way I could see all around. Three-hundred-and-sixty-degree surveillance!"

"I'll look into it tomorrow," said Hilda. "The farmhouse mystery, I mean. Not the beret periscope – I'm sorry, Alfur, but I stand out enough already without wearing a massive spy gadget on my head."

The airship passed over the city wall and floated across the Steinnharr, the sea of stones. Hilda ran to the port side of the airship and pressed her nose to the window in the hope of spotting the valley where she and her mum used to live before they moved to Trolberg. Her eyes traced the silhouettes of those dear, familiar mountains: Boot Mountain, Bottle Mountain, Mug Mountain . . .

Wait! What is that?

A huge, squat creature was galumphing down through the valley. It looked almost as tall as a forest giant, except that it was bent almost double. Its back was hideously hunched and its neck was craned forwards as if it was trying to sniff the trail in front of it. Hilda tried to make out the creature's face, but it was shrouded in a ragged hood.

A moment later, the creature disappeared, hidden from view behind Lamp Mountain. And although the Safety Patrol airship was heated to a perfect temperature, something about that shambling creature made Hilda feel horribly and inexplicably cold.

4

Inspection complete, the airship landed in a field opposite the Safety Patrol headquarters. Hilda thanked Gerda Gustav for the ride and said an awkward goodbye to Erik Ahlberg. She ran back to school through the snow, still clutching her trophy, and got there just in time for lunch break.

Frida and David sat shivering on a climbing frame in the playground. As soon as they saw her, their faces brightened.

"Look who's back!" said David. "How was your trip in the dirigible?"

"Pretty traumatic," said Hilda, "but such is the life of an adventurer."

She told them about the new bell system and about her argument with Erik Ahlberg. Then she told them about the strange farmhouse that seemed to have sprung up since that morning. Finally, she told them about the shambling, shaggy-haired monster roaming the wilderness to the north of Trolberg.

"We had an interesting morning too," said Frida. "We learned how to calculate the area of a triangle."

After school, Alfur leaped on to a passing squirrel and headed home to start work on his airship report. Hilda, David and Frida did not go home. They went to Bronstad Lane and stood on the footbridge staring at the newly appeared farmhouse.

"It doesn't look new," said Frida. "See how weather-beaten the stone is. And there's moss all over the window ledges."

"I'm telling you," said David, "this morning there was nothing here but grass. Wait, Hilda, come back!"

But Hilda was already halfway to the house. As she approached the door, she heard laughter and shouting from within, as if a party was in progress.

She lifted the heavy iron door knocker and rapped three times. When there was no answer, she turned the handle and went in.

The inside of the farmhouse was like a barn with bare stone walls and wooden floors. A funny little man in a bright red tunic was cartwheeling around. Six other men were counting in a loud chant.

"Thirty-one, thirty-two, thirty-three . . ."

As soon as they saw Hilda, they scattered. Two of them jumped in a trunk and shut the lid, two more swung themselves up into the rafters, and two dived under the bed. The last one ran to the wall, picked up a large wooden picture frame and held it up in front of his face.

Hilda went up to the picture frame and looked at the peculiar fellow. He was holding his breath, trying desperately not to blink. With his wide eyes and goofy grin, he looked kind of creepy.

"Hello," said Hilda.

The little man's arms trembled under the weight of the frame and he dropped it on the floor with a loud crash. "Scuddlebuckets!" he swore. "I knew we should have set up shop further from the city, but my mitten-brained brothers couldn't stand the extra walk."

"I'm Hilda," said Hilda. "I saw your house from the air and thought I'd come and say hello."

"I'm Kertasnikir," said the boy. "You can call me Kert. Me and my brothers here are the Thirteen Yule Lads."

The Yule Lads emerged from their hiding places and lined up beside Kert.

"There are only seven of you," said Hilda.

"We work in shifts," Kert mumbled. "Tell me something, Hilda. Are you naughty?"

The question took Hilda by surprise. "I don't think so," she said.

"You sure about that?" said a portly fellow, cartwheeling up to her. "You've never licked the burnt bits off a saucepan without permission?"

"No."

"Or slammed a door at five o'clock in the morning?" enquired a tall, bespectacled lad behind her.

"Never."

"Or whispered 'I hate you' into the ear of your gramma's woolliest sheep?" asked a pointy-eared lad hanging from a rafter.

"That's oddly specific," said Hilda. "And no, I've never done any of those things."

"What about them?" Kert pointed at Frida and David who were peering around the door, their eyes as round as rowanberries. "Are they naughty?"

"Certainly not," said Hilda. "Why all the questions?"

Kert flipped over on to his hands and pedalled his feet in the air. "It's our job to ask questions," he panted. "We Yule Lads are in charge of making sure kids get candy on the morning after the Big

Glow. But there's not enough candy for all the kids, so we skip the naughty ones."

"I see," said Hilda. "Well, if it's naughty kids you're after, come to the Winter Festival tonight. There are always plenty of troublemakers hanging around in Trolberg marketplace."

Kert flipped the right way up and pulled out a notebook and pencil. "What are their names?"

Hilda could think of at least three straight away, but she shook her head. "I'm not a telltale, Kert."

"Please!" Kert draped an arm around her shoulder. "Just one little name!"

"My lips are sealed," said Hilda.

"Suit yourself." Kert's eyes twinkled mischievously. "If you don't want to tell us plainly, why not tell us in a riddle? We Yule Lads love riddles."

Hilda considered this. She was certainly no telltale but neither did she like the thought of Trevor finding armfuls of fudge pops under the Sonstansil tree. She thought up a riddle, took a deep breath and started to sing:

"Riddle-me, riddle-me, riddle-me-ree
There's no one in Trolberg as naughty as me
My first is in TREETOP but never in GROUND
My second's in RAVEN but not in
    BLACK HOUND
My third is in DEER FOX, never in TROLL
My fourth is in VITTRA and VULTURE and VOLE
My fifth is in TREVOR but never in NEVER.
My sixth appears six-fold in TREVOR-
    TREVOR-TREVOR!"

There was a long silence, and then the Yule Lads began to talk all at the same time, bombarding her with answers.

"Ludvig!"
"Olivia!"
"Astrid!"
"Baltasar!"
"Rumplestiltskin!"

Hilda had deliberately made her riddle as easy as possible, but the more the Yule Lads guessed, the further they got from the correct answer. Besides, she could see Frida out of the corner of her eye, tapping her watch and hopping from foot to foot.

Hilda sighed. "It was nice to meet you," she told the boys, "but we have to go and set up our stall at the festival. Come down later, if you fancy some soup!"

The three friends traipsed out into the snow. Behind them, the Yule Lads carried on turning cartwheels, doing backflips and shrieking daft names to the rafters.

That night was bitterly cold and business was brisk at the Sparrow Scout Soup Stall. A long line of customers had formed in front of the cauldron and the three friends had to work fast to keep up with all the chopping, ladling and money-collecting. The profits from the sale of soup were going to the Sparrow Scouts, but there was also a tips jar on the edge of the table which Hilda was keeping a close eye on. It was filling up nicely.

"What are you going to do with your share of the tips, David?" Hilda asked, as they chopped an enormous pile of Spanish onions.

"Blow it on fudge pops, probably," said David. "What about you?"

"I'm going to buy my mum a present," said Hilda.

Hilda had been planning Mum's Big Glow present for weeks. She had noticed a while ago that whenever someone entered the flat, the draught from the door made all Mum's papers fly off her desk, so she was planning to buy her a snow globe that she could use as a paperweight.

"Hello," said a familiar voice, and Hilda looked up to see Kertasnikir standing in front of the stall, his teeth chattering.

"Kert!" she cried. "Are you here for soup?"

"Yes indeedie!" he whooped. "We all are!"

Six more Yule Lads lined up behind him, stamping and shivering in the snow. Frida ladled out seven servings of soup and passed them around. The boys chuckled as they warmed their hands on the steaming hot mugs.

"Fourteen kronor, please," said Frida, holding out her hand.

"What?" Kert paused mid-sip. "Hilda said the soup was free."

"No, she didn't," said Frida.

"Yes, she did. 'Come down to our stall if you fancy some soup,' she said. She didn't mention money."

"The clue is in the word stall," said Frida.

"But we're hungry and cold and penniless." Kert gazed from Frida to Hilda with big, innocent eyes.

Hilda hesitated for a moment, then glanced at the tips jar.

"Don't even think about it," warned Frida, realizing what her friend was about to do.

"Come on," Hilda said. "You know the Sparrow Scout oath as well as I do. Be kind to all people and animals and spir–"

"All right!" snapped Frida. "Get it over with."

Hilda counted out fourteen kronor and handed the money to Frida, leaving just two measly kronor in the tips jar.

"Thank you!" Kert blew on his soup to cool it down. "We knew you were good children the moment we saw you."

"No, you didn't," said Frida. "You asked us about five times whether we were naughty."

"We were just making conversation, weren't we, lads?"

Off the Yule Lads went, merrily sipping their soup. Hilda, Frida and David carried on serving until half past seven, when their shift ended and another group of Sparrow Scouts arrived to take over the soup stall.

Hilda went off to explore the other stalls, but doing so without any money in her pocket was very frustrating. She shielded her eyes from the neat rows of bifröst cupcakes on Madeleine's Baked Goods Stall, then hurried as fast as she could past the cuddly woffs, spinning tops and onion-scented vittra toys on Torben's Toy Stall.

"Beautiful, hand-made snow globes!" cried a voice. "Five kronor each!"

Hilda rushed over to Madame Lindgren's Gift Stall and feasted her eyes on the snow globes. Houses, trees, boats and even trolls were encased as perfect miniatures within the smooth glass balls. One of them was a handsome bludbok tree just like the ones near Hilda's old house in the wilderness. Hilda promised herself that she would earn lots of tips at the soup stall tomorrow, then come and buy this globe for Mum.

The next stall, Sandi's Sugar Shack, was a mouth-watering sight. Hilda's big eyes took in gingerbread bells, fudge pops, cotton candy, Trolberg Delight and... a skinny hand poking out of the crowd to snatch a bag of candy canes!

"Hey!" Hilda squeezed through the crowd and grabbed the candy thief by the wrist.

"I was going to pay for it!" cried a familiar voice. "I was just looking for the price tag!"

Hilda let go in surprise. "Kert!" she gasped.

The Yule Lad placed the bag of candy canes back where it belonged and grinned at Hilda sheepishly. "No harm done," he said.

Hilda glared at him with narrowed eyes.

"You were looking for naughty boys, Kertasnikir. Maybe you should look in a mirror."

"That reminds me," said Kert. "The lads and I have solved your riddle."

"Don't change the subject."

"The answer's Ingrid, isn't it?"

"Don't change the – "

"Ingrid! Ingrid! Ingrid!"

"No!"

"Give us a clue, then."

"No."

"Please?"

"No."

"Pretty please with a rowanberry on top?"

"All right," sighed Hilda. "The answer is a boy's name."

"Magnus? Alfrigg? Bodmod?"

"A boy's name beginning with T."

"Torvald? Thorbum? Turfeinar?"

"Come on!" urged Hilda. "The answer was literally in the riddle!"

"Something in the riddle beginning with T . . ." mused Kert, then suddenly his face brightened.

"TROLL!"

Hilda could have told Kert that yelling TROLL! in a crowded marketplace was a bad idea. After a moment of stunned silence, the cry was taken up by a dozen other voices and people started running to and fro.

"Troll alert!" they shouted. "Run for your lives!"

"Quick!" said Madame Lindgren to her teenage son. "Run to the Gorrill Gardens bell tower! Tell the bell-keeper to ring the bell!"

"Don't do that!" cried Hilda. "It's a misunderstanding! A false alarm! We were discussing a riddle!"

But she was too late. Already the teenager was haring off in the direction of Gorrill Gardens to deliver his message to the bell-keeper. Hilda set off after him, sprinting across the marketplace as if her life depended on it. Nothing would help Erik Ahlberg's horrible anti-troll campaign more than a city-wide troll alert, and right now only she could stop it.

6

Deep snow crunched and squeaked beneath
Hilda's boots as she chased the teenager past the
school and through the graveyard. Ahead of them
was a playground with a climbing frame and two
spindly elm trees. A line of woffs flew overhead,
their tails flickering from side to side and their big
eyes peering into the gathering gloom.

Madame Lindgren's son stopped at the gate to
Gorrill Gardens and fumbled with the latch.

"Troll alert!" he kept yelling. "Troll at Trolberg Winter Festival! Ring the bell, Mr Bell-keeper!"

As the gate swung open, Hilda tackled the boy around the waist and barrelled him to the ground. "Don't ring the bell, Mr Bell-keeper!" she shouted. "It's a false alarm! Don't ring the bell!"

But she was too late. The Gorrill Gardens bell was already swinging into action, sounding its barbaric bong over the rooftops of Trolberg. Hilda clasped her mittens over her ears as the deafening noise resounded from the mountains.

Pliff! Plaff! Pluff! A flurry of flabbergasted woffs fell all around her, raining on the snow like enormous yellow beach balls.

"Oh, you poor things!" cried Hilda. She rushed to help the stricken woffs, seizing them around their plump middles and hoisting them into the air. The woffs were a little woozy at first, but one by one they took flight and resumed their migration.

Hilda saved the biggest woff till last. With all her might she hefted it into the air, and this time she didn't let go.

When the big woff felt the weight of a human child on its back, it went completely berserk. Its eyes bulged, its ears flattened and it shot into the air like an exploding bottle-rocket. Hilda wrapped her legs around the creature's belly and clung on to its neck fur, steering up and left until she was level with the top of the bell tower.

"Thanks!" she shouted, launching herself off its back. "Oops," she added, realising that she had misjudged the dismount and was going to miss the tower completely.

Fortunately, the bell-keeper had quick reflexes. He leaned over the parapet at the top of the tower, plucked Hilda out of mid-air and hauled her to safety.

"Thank you," Hilda gasped, collapsing exhausted on to the viewing platform.

With his face in shadow beneath his hooded cloak, the bell-keeper looked like some ghastly spectre, but then he turned towards the light and Hilda saw that he was just a man with a weather-beaten brow and hairy beard.

When the bell-keeper spoke, his voice was gruff and down-to-earth. "Who are you and what do you want?"

"I'm Hilda," panted Hilda. "There's no troll, sir. It was a false alarm."

"You're sure about that?"

"One hundred per cent."

The bell-keeper heaved a sigh of relief and took a half-eaten sandwich out of his pocket. "Thank heavens," he muttered. "The last thing I want to do is to ring that shuddersome thing again."

Beyond the bell-keeper, in the shadows of the belfry, a second figure lurked beneath the bell.

"Who's your friend?" asked Hilda.

"My friend!" The bell-keeper laughed bitterly. "You think that thing's my friend? That heartless, soulless, witless gimcrack? That hodgepodge of cogs and sprockets? I am not normally a man of many words but I'll have you know, that heap of steampunk junk is definitely not my friend. It's my RIVAL, that's who it is! My NEMESIS. My despicable, mechanical, megalomaniacal ENEMY!"

"The new bell-ringer," murmured Hilda, remembering her conversation with Ahlberg.

"That's right." The bell-keeper glared at the figure in the belfry. "Thirty years I've been looking after this bell tower, and then one day I wake up and find I'm being replaced by a diesel-glugging doohickey called a Bellboy 3000. Humiliating, that's what it is!" A tear rolled down his weather-beaten face. "The Bellboy 3000 network is going to be switched on by Erik Ahlberg at a special ceremony tomorrow morning. After that, I only get to visit the tower once a week, to polish the bell and oil the mechanism. I'm done for, Hilda."

Hilda stared at the robot's hydraulic cylinders, which looked for all the world like jutting elbows. An idea stirred in the back of her mind. "What if the Bellboy 3000 got... you know... broken?" she whispered.

The bell-keeper stared at her. "Sabotaged, you mean?"

"Yes."

"You've got guts, little girl." The bell-keeper took a bite of his sandwich. "But I'm afraid the Bellboy 3000 is weatherproof, theftproof, waterproof, woffproof, bombproof, trollproof, tamperproof and shatterproof. Plus, it's wired up to forty-one other Bellboy 3000s all over the city. Plus, I don't have the blueprints that show how they're all connected. Besides, do you know the penalty for sabotaging Safety Patrol property?"

"No."

"Fifty years in Trolberg jail."

"Oh," said Hilda.

The bell-keeper forced a wry smile. "You want my advice, Hilda? Go home, get some sleep, and in the morning go straight to the Nils Pills Pharmacy and buy yourself some earplugs. You're going to need them."

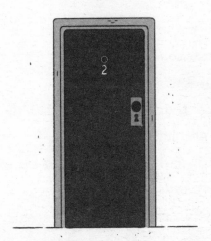

Hilda barged through the door of her building and
sprinted up the steps two at a time. As she passed
the second floor landing, the door of flat 2 opened
and an old man came out. He had a bald head,
brown skin and a bushy white beard.

"Hello, Mr Ostenfeld," said Hilda.

"Oh," said Mr Ostenfeld. "It's you."

Mr Ostenfeld did not look thrilled to see her,
but Hilda beamed back at him nevertheless. She
hardly ever saw her downstairs neighbour and this

seemed like a good opportunity to get to know him.

"I like your top," she said, pointing at his gaudy diamond-patterned cardigan. "Did your wife knit it for you?"

The old man did not reply. He began to bend down ever so slowly, reaching for a package on his doormat.

"Let me get that for you," said Hilda, grabbing the package and handing it to him. It was wrapped in brown paper and it was heavy, like a stack of magazines or catalogues.

Mr Ostenfeld turned to go back inside, then stopped and looked at Hilda with sadness in his eyes. "I don't have a wife," he said. "And anyway, I'm perfectly capable of knitting my own cardigans."

"Sorry," said Hilda.

"It's not your fault," said Mr Ostenfeld, closing the door. "Your mother should have taught you not to ask personal questions."

Hilda remained on the landing, deep in thought, then went on up to her own flat. "Hi, Mum, I'm home!" she cried, flinging open the front door and pulling off her boots. The flat was toasty warm despite the snow outside, and a divine aroma of ginger, nutmeg and caraway seeds wafted over her.

"Hi, Hilda!" Mum gathered her papers off the floor and plonked them back on her desk. "How was the airship?"

"Fine."

"And school?"

"Fine."

"And the Sparrow Scout Soup Stall?"

"Fine."

"Glad to hear it," said Mum. She went into the kitchen and came back with two baguettes and two steaming bowls of stew. "Are you excited about the Big Glow tomorrow night?"

"Very." Hilda seized a baguette and bit an enormous chunk off the end. "Though I wish the Wood Man were here to celebrate with us."

"I don't think the Wood Man is the celebrating type," Mum chuckled.

"I still miss him sometimes," said Hilda. "Just like I miss our little cabin in the wilderness and our open fire and playing Dragon Panic after dinner and – hey, let's play Dragon Panic after dinner!"

Mum shook her head. "I'd love to, darling, but I have to work. My new commission is driving me crazy. Would you believe it, those boffins at SPHQ sent me more than a hundred pages of reference material!"

Hilda grunted and dunked a piece of bread in her casserole.

"I'm only designing a couple of posters and a backdrop for a speech," continued Mum. "Do I want a whole sheaf of schematic diagrams for some unfathomable, hare-brained contraption? No, sirree, I really don't."

Hilda made sympathetic noises through mouthfuls of baguette.

After dinner, Mum went back to her drawing table and Hilda curled up on the sofa with Twig, a mug of hot chocolate and Emil Gammelplassen's new book, *Cities and their Unfriendly Occupants*. Gammelplassen was no fan of cities, especially since running into a barghest on his last visit to Trolberg.

Hilda was in the middle of a rather alarming

chapter about nightmare spirits when Twig suddenly pricked up his ears and growled.

"What is it, boy?" said Hilda. "What can you hear? Do you think it's a nightmare spirit?"

Twig sprinted lippety-clippety along the hallway to Hilda's bedroom. Hilda followed, still carrying her mug of hot chocolate, eager to see what had startled him.

Standing on the ledge outside Hilda's bedroom window was a pigeon with beady orange eyes. Mounted on the pigeon's back was Bartel Braga, the wildest elf in all of Trolberg, dressed in full battle armour and tapping the windowpane with the end of his spear.

Hilda opened the window and let him in. "Nice to see you," she said.

"Nasty emu?" said Bartel. "That's no way to talk about Cedric. I know he's on the big side for a pigeon, but–"

"I said, it's nice to see you," said Hilda. "Some hot chocolate?"

"Sir Lancelot?" The bearded elf looked confused. "No, Giant Girl. Underneath this shining

armour, I'm just plain old Bartel Braga."

"Alfur, are you here?" called Hilda. "We could do with some help."

Alfur Aldric emerged from his hiding place in Hilda's pencil case. The Aldrics and the Bragas were no longer sworn enemies, but Alfur was still a little nervous of those strange, wild elves who lived in cracks in the city wall and spent their days making silk and practising their jousting skills.

"Alfur," said Hilda. "I want you to write three notes for our friend. Number one, nice to see you. Number two, would you like some hot chocolate? Number three, you seem to have a problem with your hearing."

Alfur scribbled the messages and showed them to Braga.

"I do indeed," said Braga. "My ears have been ringing like crazy ever since that first Big Bong. I can't hear very well at all!"

"I guessed," said Hilda.

"Agnes?" said Bartel. "Don't you worry about Ancient Agnes. She's been hard of hearing for twenty-five years, that one. No, it's the rest of us

I'm worried about. Our rabbit steeds have all run off. Our babies have stopped sleeping. The lids of our pickled onion jars keep shooting into the air like champagne corks, and as for the silkworms, you don't even want to know what happened to them on that second Bong. Made quite a mess, I can tell you."

"You should see what it's doing to woffs," said Hilda.

"To what?"

"To woffs."

"To what?"

"TO WOFFS!" yelled Hilda. "TO MIGRATING WOFFS!"

"Poor things," said Bartel. "Sensitive creatures, moths, especially when they're ice skating."

Hilda sat down on her bed and rested her chin in her hands, thinking furiously. Twig jumped into her lap and gazed at her with glistening black eyes.

"It's no good you two sitting there pouting like huldermaids," snapped Bartel. "If they're going to keep bonging like that, then we need to band together and declare war. War on the bell towers!"

"War on the bell towers!" cried Alfur, punching the air with a stubby arm. "Terms and conditions may apply," he added in a quieter voice.

"Coo-roo-catoo!" called Cedric the pigeon from his perch on the window ledge.

All eyes were now on Hilda.

"I don't want to declare war," she said. "What if we tried some strenuous non-violent resistance instead?"

"I suppose we could try it," said Bartel, looking a little disappointed. "It won't be easy, though. For a start, we don't have any idea how those new mechanical bell-ringers are connected to each other. If only we had some paperwork – schematic diagrams or something."

Hilda looked up sharply. For one thing, it was a surprise to hear a Braga elf wishing he had some paperwork. For another, this was the second time tonight that she had heard the phrase schematic diagrams.

"Alfur," she asked, "what do the letters SPHQ stand for?"

"Safety Patrol Headquarters."

Hilda leaped up so fast she banged her head on the shelf above her bed. "That's it!" she cried. "Mum's new commission! She's designing posters for the Safety Patrol. She was complaining just now that they sent her too much paperwork."

"No such thing," sniffed Alfur.

"She's got the... schem-whatever diagrams for the new bells!" said Hilda. "They're on her desk."

Bartel rubbed his hands together. "So, which one of us is going to go and pinch them?"

"I am," said a determined voice, and a fuzzball with an enormous nose slid out from underneath Hilda's bed.

A lifetime of purloining unloved and unwanted objects had made Tontu the house spirit an expert pilferer. He slid back under Hilda's bed and returned a few moments later with the blueprints for the new bell system.

"That was quick!" gasped Hilda, who was still getting used to the idea that all the hidden places in her house were mysteriously interconnected.

Tontu shrugged. "She was fast asleep at her desk. It was like taking candy from a baby – only less mean."

8

The planning meeting took place at midnight on the roof of David's house. The whole gang was present: Frida, David, Alfur, Tontu and Twig, with Bartel Braga and Cedric the pigeon. They sat in a circle, faces smeared with chimney soot, the bell tower blueprints in the middle.

"Thank you all for coming," whispered Hilda. "And thank you, Tontu, for bringing me and Twig here through Nowhere Space."

"Use your bike next time," muttered Tontu. "Nowhere Space is not for everyday travel."

"Let's get down to business," said Hilda. "This is the first meeting of Operation Deer Fox Thunder Team."

"Wait, what?" David goggled at her.

"Our code name," whispered Hilda, as if it was obvious. "Now, the bad news is that the new mechanical bell-ringer system will be activated tomorrow morning. That means bigger, louder bells in all forty-two bell towers, automated to ring every fifteen minutes." She paused while a horrified shudder rippled through the group. "The good news is, we can stop it from happening. Isn't that right, Frida?"

"That's right." Frida unfolded a map of Trolberg and spread it out beside the Bellboy 3000 schematics. "I have identified a weak point in their system. According to these blueprints, all of the mechanical bell-ringers are controlled from one central bell tower – here." She stabbed her finger on to the map in the middle of the Financial District. "This bell tower is nicknamed the Bottle

Opener because of the shape of its belfry. If we sneak inside the tower and cut the correct cable, the whole system goes down."

David raised a pair of binoculars to his eyes and tracked across the Trolberg skyline until he spotted the Bottle Opener. "Sneak inside?" he quavered. "It's crawling with workers and guards."

"Don't worry," grinned Hilda. "We'll do it during tomorrow's Switching-on Ceremony, while everyone is listening to Erik Ahlberg's speech. Frida will now demonstrate the plan using Dragon Panic pieces."

Frida cleared her throat and held up a small, metal warrior. "David, this is you," she said, positioning him on the map. "You will be stationed as a lookout on the roof of Flimflåm Bank."

David paled under his covering of soot. "Flimflåm Bank is even taller than the Bottle Opener!" he gasped. "And it's not so much a roof as a pointy pinnacle!"

Frida ignored David's objection and picked two dragons out of the box. "Bartel, this orange dragon represents you and your pigeon-riders. You will attack the Bottle Opener from the air to distract the guards near the top. And the green dragon here is Ancient Agnes. She will lead the ground assault. Alfur, you will be Agnes's eyes and ears. Make sure she's facing in the right direction at all times."

Bartel chuckled and slapped Alfur on the back. "How about that?" he cried. "Bragas and Aldrics, brothers in arms!"

Alfur smiled weakly. He looked as if he was about to be sick.

"As for you, Tontu," said Frida, "you will use Nowhere Space to get me and Hilda into the control room of the tower. Don't tut, Tontu. You wouldn't say that sabotaging a network of mechanical bell-ringers was 'everyday travel', would you?"

"All right, I'll do it," said Tontu. "One last time, all right?"

"Thank you, Tontu." Hilda beamed. "Well, once we're inside the control room, the rest is easy-peasy. We'll find this... er... RJ64 patch cable and we'll cut it with a pair of Sparrow Scout cable cutters. Snippety-snip, no more mechanical bell-ringers!"

The plotters grinned and high-fived each other, except for Twig, who let out a little What-About-Me? whimper.

"Twig, you'll be with me," said Hilda, pulling him close. "You're my bodyguard!"

"Planning phase complete," said Frida. "Now, let's all put our hands in the middle of the circle and yell OPERATION DEER FOX THUNDER TEAM IS GO!"

"Could we whisper it?" said David. "It's just that my parents are really light sleepers."

"Fine," said Frida. "One... two... three..."

"Operation Deer Fox Thunder Team is GO!" they all murmured.

9

The day of the ceremony dawned like a picture postcard. Frost glittered on the windows of Trolberg Town Hall and a fresh fall of snow blanketed its roof.

A stage had been set up in front of the town hall. On it stood a lectern, a microphone and an enormous switch marked 'Bellboy 3000'.

As Hilda took her seat in the stands, a kaleidoscope of butterflies fluttered in her stomach. Last night it had seemed that Operation Deer Fox Thunder Team could not possibly fail. Now, in the cold light of day, it seemed it could not possibly succeed.

"Look," said Mum. "They're unveiling my artwork."

An enormous canvas at the back of the stage was being unfurled from top to bottom. Hilda stared at it. In the middle of the picture, gleaming like a colossal golden idol, was a mechanical bell-ringer. Down at the bottom were the inky silhouettes of fleeing trolls.

"Well?" asked Mum. "What do you think?"

"Very dramatic," said Hilda.

The Trolberg Choir filed on to the stage and began to sing a song called 'Sweet Pealing Bells':

'Sweet pealing bells, jubilant they knell
Swinging in the tower every quarter hour...'

Hilda felt a tap on the shoulder, and turned to see Kertasnikir in the seat behind her.

"The lads and I have solved your riddle," Kert beamed. "It's Trevor, isn't it?"

"Well done," said Hilda. "You got there in the end." The walkie-talkie in her coat pocket emitted a loud crackle.

Mum looked at her. "What was that noise?"

"Tummy rumbling," replied Hilda. "I guess I must be hungry."

"But you just ate three enormous pancakes and half a tin of syrup."

"All the same," said Hilda, "I should probably get some doughnuts from the food van. Would you like some?"

"No, thank you," said Mum primly.

"Yes, please," said Kert, but Hilda was already out of her seat and edging her way along the row.

'Sweet pealing bells, jubilant they knell
Swinging in the tower every quarter hour...'

"Blue, this is Bugman." David's voice crackled from the walkie-talkie. "I'm in position. Over."

Hilda glanced up at Flimflåm Bank, a shining cucumber of glass and aluminium, and spotted a terrified speck clinging to the mast at the top of the building.

Good old David, she thought.

She hurried past the Nils Pills Pharmacy and

turned left into a quiet alley. Frida and Tontu stepped out of the shadows, holding walkie-talkies.

Hilda raised her own walkie-talkie to her mouth. "Bugman, this is Blue," she said. "I'm with Badges and Hairball. Do you have eyes on the Invisibles? Over."

"Invisibles in position," said David. "Bartel and Agnes look ready for battle, and Alfur... well, Alfur looks how I feel. Over."

"Wait for Big Cheese to begin his speech," said Hilda. "Then give the signal to attack. Over and out."

Hilda could not see the stage from the alley, but she could hear well enough.

The song 'Sweet Pealing Bells' came to an end and was replaced by the nasal, lilting voice of Erik Ahlberg.

"Friends, Trolbergians, countrypeople!" he began. "Thank you for joining us on this momentous day, the most momentous day since my illustrious ancestor, Edmund Ahlberg, erected Trolberg's very first bell tower. On that day, like today, the people decided to do something about

the terrible threat encroaching on their borders.
And on that day, like today, a mighty hero arose
to lead them in their struggle..."

Frida looked at her watch. "It's time," she said.

Hilda lifted the walkie-talkie to her mouth.
"Bugman, this is Blue. Signal the Invisibles to
begin their attack. Over."

"Roger that, Blue. Over and out."

Twig jumped up and wriggled into Hilda's
adventuring satchel. Tontu took her and Frida by
the hand and stepped backwards into the mouth
of a drainpipe. The alleyway swirled around
Hilda's head and collapsed in on her like a
broken umbrella.

SHOOP!

Frida looked around in amazement. "So this is
Nowhere Space. It's messy, isn't it?"

"No time for idle chit-chat," said Tontu. "Follow
me!" He led the girls along the tunnel, around a
bend and up a wobble-walled slope.

When he reached the top, he swan-dived gracefully through a glowing hole.

Frida hesitated, staring at the hole. "I've got a bad feeling about this," she stammered.

Hilda was just about to push Frida through the hole when Tontu reappeared, coughing and spluttering. "Wrong portal," he said. "That one comes out in a public toilet."

"Eew!" exclaimed the girls.

"Let us never speak of it again," said Tontu. He stepped to his right and dived through a different hole.

Hilda grabbed Frida's hand.

"We'll go together," she said. "One... two... three... JUMP!"

10

If there had been any security guards in the
control room of the Bottle Opener bell tower,
they would have been astonished to see a house
spirit and two Sparrow Scouts roll out of a
communications cabinet on to the floor. But at
that moment, the Bottle Opener's security guards
were all up near the top of the tower, attempting to
fend off two platoons of invisible elves.

The control room was crammed with humming
machines, blinking lights, and tier upon tier
of tangled wires. Twig sprang out of Hilda's
adventuring satchel and scampered around the
room, checking for threats. As for Tontu, he wished
them luck and returned to Nowhere Space.

Frida bent over the Bellboy 3000 schematics. "According to this," she said, "the RJ64 patch cable is in tier three of cabinet 27."

Finding tier three of cabinet 27 was easy, but finding the right wire was not. Hilda opened her Sparrow Scout cable cutters and frowned at the horrifying spaghetti of thick wires, thin wires, copper wires, tin wires, graded wires, braided wires and wayward every-which-way wires.

"Which do I cut?" she asked.

Frida peered again at the schematic diagram. "I'm going to say . . . all of them. Just to be on the safe side."

As Hilda set to work with the cable cutters, the walkie-talkie crackled into life. "Blue and Badges, this is Bugman. Big Cheese just said 'in conclusion', so I'm guessing his speech is nearly over. Over."

"We're out of time!" cried Frida. "Give me those!" She grabbed the cable cutters from Hilda and began to wrench great handfuls of wires out of the cabinet, slashing and slicing as if her life depended on it.

One bright yellow cable looked a little thicker than the others, and when Frida snipped it a series of clicks and clunks sounded from deep inside the cabinet.

"System offline," said a computerized voice.

"You did it!" Hilda hugged her friend from behind. "Well done, Frida!"

"Initiating backup system," said the computerized voice.

Frida flinched. "Say, what?"

"Backup system initiated." The computer sounded positively smug. "System online."

Frida rifled through the Bellboy 3000 schematics. "Of course!" She stabbed the diagram with a frantic finger. "When the RJ64 miscarries, the bias on the tunnel diode is instantly reversed, activating the backup system way up at the top of the bell tower."

"I don't understand!" cried Hilda.

"You don't need to understand." Frida pressed the cable cutters into Hilda's right hand. "You just need to sprint up three hundred steps in less than a minute. You can do it, Hilda. You're faster than I am."

Hilda ran for the door, Twig bounding at her heels.

"Find the control booth and cut the master wire!" yelled Frida.

"Roger that!" cried Hilda, and she flung herself up the spiral steps three at a time, counting in her head – three, six, nine, twelve, fifteen, eighteen . . .

Erik Ahlberg's voice echoed through the tower. "Before I flick this switch," he was saying, "let me pay tribute to the bell-keepers of Trolberg. They always tried their best, poor fellows, and for that we are grateful. But over the years we have watched them grow old and slow. No aggression! No sense of urgency! No fizz! No pizazz! No oomph!"

Seventy-two, seventy-five, seventy-eight, eighty-one . . . When Hilda lived in the wilderness with no one but Mum and Twig for company, she often used to run in the foothills of Boot Mountain. Her heart was big. Her lungs were fit. Her legs were strong.

"Just last month," continued Ahlberg, "I saw a mother troll gathering mushrooms outside the city wall. And what did the bell-keeper do about it? He leaned out of his belfry and tried to shoo the troll away by flapping his hands and hissing!"

One hundred and forty-one, one hundred and forty-four, one hundred and forty-seven . . .

"And when the old codger finally came to his senses and rang the bell, what do you think the troll did? Did it squirm and clutch its ears? Did it drop its basket and flee for the hills?"

One hundred and ninety-two, one hundred and ninety-five, one hundred and ninety-eight . . .

"No, it did not! It sniffed the air, picked its panhandle nose and went on gathering mushrooms. Citizens of Trolberg, if we get any kinder and gentler in this city, we will cease to exist!"

Two hundred and ten, two hundred and thirteen, two hundred and sixteen . . . Hilda passed a balcony where four hapless security guards were being dive-bombed by invisible warriors on pigeons. The guards were so distracted they did not notice a blue-haired saboteur and her deer fox friend careering up the steps.

"We used to have victories!" cried Ahlberg.

"We don't have victories any more!"

Two hundred and fifty-five, two hundred and fifty-eight, two hundred and sixty-one. Hilda's legs were aching now, and her breath came in short ragged gasps.

"We need to start winning again! It's time to restore our city to its former greatness."

Two hundred and ninety-four, two hundred and ninety-seven, THREE HUNDRED! Hilda burst through a trapdoor into the open air and looked around her wildly.

"Ladies and gentlemen, I present to you the Bellboy 3000! You heard one of the new bells yesterday, but when I flick this switch you will hear all forty-two bells ringing in unison!"

Beside the belfry was a metal door marked CONTROL BOOTH, SAFETY PATROL ONLY. Hilda threw herself at the door and wrenched the handle up and down.

It was locked.

"It all comes down to this," Ahlberg declared. "The flick of one little switch by one mighty finger!"

"Move aside," said a gruff voice.

Peering through the eyeholes of her mask, Hilda saw a hooded figure looming over her. "You!" she gasped.

The bell-keeper reached out and slipped a small, golden key into the lock.

"You're helping us!" stammered Hilda. "Why?"

"I couldn't let myself be shown up by a child," said the bell-keeper. "Plus, Ahlberg just called me an old codger."

The key turned. The door swung open. Hilda dashed into the control booth. "Where's the master wire?" she cried.

"Behind this panel. Do you have a screwdriver?"

"No."

"A coin?"

"No!"

In the belfry next to them, the mechanical bell-ringer began to stir.

"He flicked the switch!" the bell-keeper groaned. "All forty-two bells across the city are cranking up! We're too late!"

"We can't be!" cried Hilda. "There must be something we can do!"

"There is." The bell-keeper reached for two pairs of ear protectors. "We can cover our ears."

11

Even with the aid of ear protectors, the new bells were eye-poppingly, mind-meldingly, ear-splittingly loud. At the top of the Bottle Opener, Hilda and the bell-keeper gaped at each other in pure horror. Down below, the people of Trolberg wailed and clutched their ears. Several flocks of migrating woffs tumbled head over tail towards the ground.

At the mouth of a cave on the upper slopes of Mount Halldór, a two-headed troll began to beat its chest in rage. It summoned another, bigger troll and the two of them made their way down the mountainside towards the city. It was just as Hilda had imagined. The trolls were not fleeing. They were getting riled.

Hilda watched the immense bell swinging frenziedly back and forth in its belfry. Any louder, she thought, and that thing will fly right off its hinges!

The thought sparked an idea – an idea so far-fetched it just might work. Hilda reached for the control panel and grabbed the VOLUME dial in both hands.

"What are you playing at?" mouthed the bell-ringer.

"I'm going to put this bad boy through its paces!" yelled Hilda, and she twisted the dial all the way up into the red 'danger' zone.

The bells swung even higher.

The bells rang even louder.

Bell towers all across Trolberg shuddered from belfry to base.

"Hang on tight!" shrieked Hilda.

Sparks flew from the control panel in front of her, the mechanical bell-ringer burst into flame and the thirty-tonne bell flew right off its moorings.

"Duck!" yelled the bell-keeper.

The gargantuan bell flew over their heads, smashed through the wall of the control booth and plummeted towards the ground. It landed with an almighty bong, then fell on its side and started to roll.

Like a runaway wrecking ball, the bell careered through the town square towards the Trolberg Choir, who dived out of the way with tuneful yawps of terror. Finally, the bell veered left, hit a kerb and flipped up on end, neatly imprisoning Head Officer Erik Ahlberg:

KLONNGGGGGG!

There followed a long, eerie silence. Hilda and the bell-keeper staggered to their feet and stared out through the hole created by the breakaway bell.

Forty-two plumes of dark smoke spiralled into the air from the ravaged bell towers, but some things were already returning to normal. Woffs resumed their migration. Trolls returned to their caves. Somewhere, a bird began to sing.

CHAPTER ELEVEN

"What do you think that is?" said the bell-keeper.

"Sounds like a robin," said Hilda.

"Not the bird – that!"

Hilda followed the bell-keeper's quivering finger and saw the same shaggy, hunchbacked creature that she had glimpsed from the airship. It was much closer to Trolberg now, shambling among the standing stones of the Steinnharr. Hilda noticed two stubby, misshapen prongs poking out of the top of the creature's head like the antlers of a forest giant.

But this was no forest giant. It looked like something much more sinister – some sort of ogre, perhaps. As Hilda gazed at the peculiar creature, goosebumps prickled on her skin.

"I'm not scared of that," Hilda muttered.

Hilda and Twig left the bell tower and mingled with the crowds in front of the town hall. A circle of children had formed around the Bottle Opener bell, and Deputy Gerda was making valiant attempts to lift it.

"Put your back into it, Gerda!" a nasal voice

echoed from inside the bell. "Lift from the knees! Come on!"

Mum pressed through the crowd and gathered Hilda into her arms. "Darling! Are you all right?"

"I'm fine," said Hilda. "Sorry I took a long time, Mum, but the line at the doughnut van was insane. I say line, but it was more of a mêlée, really. Sixty people, all trying to get to the front. And you'll never believe what happened when I reached the serving window. They had run out of doughnut mixture!"

Mum's expression hardened. "You're right," she said. "I don't believe you."

"Huh?"

"Hilda, I saw you at the top of the bell tower!" Mum lowered her voice to a tearful whisper. "If you had come down here and told me the truth, I might even have forgiven you. But no, it wasn't enough for you to sabotage Safety Patrol property and risk fifty years in jail, was it? You thought you'd hurt me even more by lying to my face!"

Hilda gulped. She picked up Twig and hugged him tight against her cheek. The two of them gazed up at Mum with big, round eyes.

"Don't even try that cutesy stuff on me!" Mum's voice trembled with fury. "You're grounded until further notice and that's final."

Hilda lay on her bed, cuddling a woff toy and glaring at the ceiling. A cucumber sandwich and two hardboiled eggs lay untouched on her bedside table. Mum had brought Hilda's supper up to her room before heading back out to the Trolberg Winter Festival.

Hilda was furious. Being grounded meant missing the soup stall, her last chance to earn tips. It also meant missing the Big Glow, which she had been so looking forward to.

Mum's loss, of course. No snow globe for her this year.

"Cheer up," said Alfur, who had hitched a ride home on Twig's back. "Operation Deer Fox Thunder Team was a great success, thanks to you."

"That's just it," said Hilda. "Mum should be thanking me for saving Trolberg from all-out war with the trolls. And instead, what does she do? She glares at me like I'm a slug in her salad, locks me in my room and flounces off to the Winter Festival without me. Don't laugh, Alfur, it's not funny."

"I didn't laugh," Alfur whispered. "I think the laughter came from the window ledge."

Hilda whipped her head around. She glimpsed a flash of movement at the edge of the window, then nothing but dark sky.

Ever so slowly she got to her feet and tiptoed across the floor. Ever so slowly she reached for the window latch. Quick as a snake strike, she flung open the window and shot out her hand.

"Gotcha!" she cried, closing her fingers. "Alfur, I've caught a thief!"

12

A little man in a floppy hat teetered into view along the edge of the window ledge. "I'm not a thief!" he cried, trying to yank his coat tails out of Hilda's grasp. "I'm Gluggagaegir."

"You're one of those pesky Yule Lads," said Hilda, still holding tight to the boy's coat tails. "What are you doing on my window ledge?"

"Looking through your window," said Gluggagaegir. "It's nothing weird," he added, seeing the expression on Hilda's face. "I look through windows in the hope of spotting unattended food. A steaming hot pie on a windowsill, a chocolate cake on a sideboard . . ."

"A cucumber sandwich on a bedside table?"

"Exactly."

"So you are a thief," said Hilda.

"Yes, but only food."

"I'll give you the cucumber sandwich," said Hilda, *"on condition that you NEVER peep at anyone's window EVER again, EVER."*

"Deal," said Gluggagaegir.

Hilda fetched the sandwich and the Yule Lad wolfed it down. "Can I ask you something?" he said, with a sly twinkle in his eyes. "Have you by any chance been shut in your room because of your naughtiness?"

"No," said Hilda. "Because of Mum's naughtiness."

"What?" Gluggagaegir looked astonished. "You mean to say, grown-ups can be naughty?"

"My mum can," said Hilda, warming to her theme. "First, she designed a bunch of posters for that awful Ahlberg man, and then she got mad at me for successfully preventing a war. If that's not ultra-naughty, I don't know what is."

Gluggagaegir took a dog-eared notebook from his pocket and scribbled eagerly. "I can't wait to tell the boys," he chuckled. "They are going to be so excited!" And with that, he bowed low, leaped on to the drainpipe and slid out of sight.

Hilda watched him go. She was still looking down when her downstairs neighbour Mr Ostenfeld came out on to his balcony. He was still wearing his diamond-patterned cardigan, and was holding the parcel that Hilda had handed him earlier.

"What do you think it is, Alfur?" whispered Hilda.

"Looks like it could be paperwork," said Alfur reverently.

Mr Ostenfeld ripped the parcel open and took out a stack of magazines. Hilda and Alfur watched him as he lifted the top one off the pile and opened it.

Hilda had seen plenty of strange things in her life – a car flying through Nowhere Space, a transmogrifying raven, a giant as big as a mountain – but what she saw next went right to the top of her list of Strange Things I Have Seen. The moment Mr Ostenfeld opened his magazine, he disappeared into thin air – then reappeared a second later as if nothing had happened. He sighed, put the magazine down on a plastic table and went inside.

"Gah!" cried Hilda. "Did you see that?"

"A disappearing neighbour," said Alfur. "Or maybe it was just us blinking."

"It wasn't us blinking," said Hilda. "It was something to do with the magazine. He disappeared the moment he opened it."

"Wait a second," said Alfur. "You just got mad at a Yule Lad for spying at windows and now we're doing the same ourselves!"

"This is not spying," said Hilda. "This is investigating."

She opened her bedroom window and climbed out on to the drainpipe. Mum would be at the Winter Festival for at least two hours. Plenty of time to find out what was going on with Mr Ostenfeld.

"I'm sorry," said Alfur, "but I can't let you go. Mum made me sign a pledge to tell her if you left the building."

"I'm not leaving the building," said Hilda. "I'm going downstairs by means of the drainpipe, which is part of the building."

"Good loophole." Alfur climbed up into her ear. "In that case, I'll come too."

Hilda slid down the drainpipe, jumped sideways and landed softly on Mr Ostenfeld's balcony. Judging from the clatter of pots and pans inside the flat, it sounded like Mr Ostenfeld was cooking.

Hilda ducked down behind the plastic table and picked up the magazine Mr Ostenfeld had been reading – the December 1947 issue of Elan magazine. She opened it, half expecting something magical to happen, but nothing did.

Hilda put down the magazine and picked another from the stack. This one was also Elan magazine, December 1947.

"Strange," she whispered. "Why do you think Mr Ostenfeld has ordered multiple copies of the same – "

VOOP!

Hilda opened the magazine and her surroundings changed in an instant.

"Gah!" she exclaimed for the second time that night. She was no longer on Mr Ostenfeld's shabby concrete balcony. She was on an ornate marble veranda surrounded by expensive-looking potted plants and wicker armchairs. The clatter of pots and pans was gone and in its place the sound of silk-smooth jazz bejewelled the air.

The magazine fell from Hilda's fingers and –

VOOP!

she was back on Mr Ostenfeld's balcony.

"Well, that was traumatic." she said out loud. "I feel kind of dizzy."

"So, you're back are you?" The sliding door of the flat flew open, and out on to the balcony strode Mr Ostenfeld. "You used one of my magazines, didn't you? You went back to 1947! How could you do such a thing?"

Hilda was alarmed by Mr Ostenfeld's tone of voice, but she could see no escape route.

The balcony rails hemmed her in on every side.

"The magazines!" hissed Alfur.

"Open another magazine."

As Mr Ostenfeld advanced towards her with his arms outstretched, Hilda lunged for a copy of Elan.

VOOP!

13

Hilda was back on the sumptuous marble balcony. The night air smelled sweet and fresh, devoid of noxious car fumes. Hilda rolled up the magazine and stuffed it into her pocket to keep it open. She had no intention of returning to Mr Ostenfeld's balcony just yet.

The smooth strains of a jazz saxophone steadied her beating heart. She pushed aside a rose-print curtain and stepped through the balcony door into a dim-lit jazz café. Couples danced. Musicians played. Candles in silver candelabras threw flickering shapes across the crimson wallpaper.

"I'm telling Mum," said Alfur. "You've definitely left your building now."

"Don't be daft," said Hilda. "I wasn't grounded in 1947, was I?"

Alfur considered this. "Another excellent loophole," he sighed. "I feel strangely proud of you."

Hilda's eyes were drawn to one young couple dancing among the tables. They were doing an energetic, jittery sort of dance involving lots of swaying of hips, kicking of feet and twirling back and forth. Their arms kept getting tangled up with each other and a couple of times the young man accidentally kicked the woman in the shins, but somehow the couple's clumsiness only added to their charm. They were laughing, joking and having a whale of a time.

"Stop right there!" hissed an angry voice. Hilda whirled around to see Mr Ostenfeld looming over her wearing a scowl that could fell a troll.

"I'm sorry – " she began, but Mr Ostenfeld was no longer listening. He was distracted by the dancing couple and his scowl had already been replaced by a soppy, faraway expression.

"She was so beautiful," he murmured.

Hilda looked from the old man to the young man and back again. Both men had handsome dark eyes under bushy eyebrows.

"It's you!" she exclaimed. "That's you in 1947, isn't it?"

Mr Ostenfeld swallowed hard and wiped away a tear. "Happiest night of my life," he croaked. "I was twenty-three years old, sitting at the bar, reading Elan magazine, when along she came and spilled her drink all over me."

"On purpose?"

"No, of course not on purpose," Mr Ostenfeld snapped. "She was a little clumsy, that's all. One of her many adorable qualities."

Hilda did not think clumsiness was adorable, but she let it pass. "What happened then?" she asked.

"We got talking. We chatted about the Winter Lore feature in my magazine and then suddenly she asked me if I liked dancing, and I said no, and she said why not, and I said I usually end up kicking someone, and she said, 'Don't worry, I'm wearing shin pads.' "

"And was she?" asked Hilda. "Wearing shin pads, I mean."

"No, of course she wasn't." Mr Ostenfeld glared at Hilda.

Hilda looked at the young woman twirling on the dance floor, her stockinged legs kicking back and forth.

"So the shin pads line was just her way of asking you to dance?"

"Yes," said Mr Ostenfeld. "We danced all night, even the slower, more romantic dances, and then–" He broke off suddenly and wiped a tear from his cheek. "I never saw her again."

"Why not?" asked Hilda. "Did you forget to ask for her address?"

"Of course I didn't forget!" yelled Mr Ostenfeld, so loudly that everyone in the club turned to look at him. "Sorry," he said, sitting down at a table and lowering his voice. "No, I didn't forget. I desperately wanted to ask for her address, but I couldn't pluck up the courage to do it. I was shy, you see. Hopelessly, incurably, idiotically shy. And when the music ended, we fetched our coats and went our separate ways. I never even got her name."

Hilda sat and watched the young couple dancing. They seemed such a good match for each other, she could hardly believe they had only just met. To think how happy they might have been if they had only stayed in touch.

"Sorry to interrupt this bittersweet moment," said Alfur in her ear, "but you really need to look behind you."

Hilda turned and looked.

"Gah!" she gasped for the third time that night. She leaped to her feet, the magazine fell out of her pocket and –

VOOP!

– she was back on Mr Ostenfeld's balcony. Mr Ostenfeld reappeared beside her. "What's wrong?" he asked.

"I'll tell you what's wrong!" cried Hilda, her voice trembling. "There were seven copies of you sitting at the table right behind us!"

"Of course there were." Mr Ostenfeld shrugged his shoulders. "That was my eighth visit to the club, so the seven previous versions of me were all there too. Think about it."

Hilda thought about it and began to feel a little calmer. "They all looked so sad," she said at last.

"Just sitting there, dreaming about what might have been."

"Welcome to my life," said Mr Ostenfeld wistfully. "Ever since that night, I've done nothing but dream. When they closed the jazz club and converted it into flats, I bought one so I could still feel close to her. And then last year I saw an advertisement to send away for copies of old magazines. I ordered the one I was reading that night, and when I opened it..."

"Voop," Hilda murmured. "Do you know how the magic works?"

"No idea," said Mr Ostenfeld. "All I know is, each copy of the magazine only works once. I have to keep ordering more, so that I can see her whenever I want – even though it means watching her slip through my fingers over and over again."

"And have you ever tried to, you know, change things?"

Mr Ostenfeld's eyes widened. "Certainly not," he said. "The past is the past. Who knows what horrifying consequences might result from trying to change it?"

"But it's already horrifying!" cried Hilda. "All those different versions of you sitting at that table with tragic, grief-lined faces! You've got to do something, Mr Ostenfeld. If you don't, I will!"

An unpleasant burning smell wafted through the open door. "Oops," the old man muttered. "I left the oven on when I came out here earlier. My sausages will be frazzled to a crisp."

As her neighbour hurried indoors to rescue his dinner, Hilda seized her chance. She picked up the last magazine and opened it.

VOOP!

She arrived on the balcony just in time to see two identical copies of herself appear out of thin air. One of them gasped, dropped her magazine and disappeared. The other one rolled up her magazine, stuffed it in her pocket and ventured inside looking nervous but determined.

"This is too weird for words," Hilda muttered, following her previous self into the club.

She left her previous self on the dance floor and made her way to the back of the room. She helped herself to a handful of peanuts from the bar, then sat down at a corner table and blew out the candle.

The saxophone lowed, the piano tinkled and the love-struck young couple danced the night away. Hilda's eyelids grew heavy. Her head lolled forwards on to her arm. Such sweet music...

14

"Miss, it's closing time. You need to go."

Hilda's head jerked up off her arm.

"Huh? What?"

A waiter was leaning over her. When he saw her face, he looked surprised. "How old are you?" he asked. "How did you get in here?"

For a moment, Hilda herself didn't know the answer to that, but she soon remembered. "Where are they?" she cried, pushing past the waiter and running for the door. "Mr Ostenfeld! Get her address!"

Hilda barged through the front door of the club

and bounded down the steps on to the pavement. The young Mr Ostenfeld was standing in the rain gazing down the street with a forlorn expression. His hair was plastered to his forehead and his white shirt was soaked to the skin.

"Mr Ostenfeld," Hilda panted. "Ask for her name and address – quick!"

The young man sprang back alarmed. "Where did you come from?" he cried. "How do you know my name? Why is your hair blue?"

"None of that is important," said Hilda. "The crucial thing right now is to run after that girl and make plans to see her again."

"Funny," Mr Ostenfeld murmured. "I was just thinking the exact same thing." He peered at Hilda through the raindrops dripping from his eyelashes, then turned and squinted down the road at the distant figure of the young woman he had been dancing with.

"Go after her, Mr Ostenfeld!" shouted Hilda. "If you don't, you'll regret it for the rest of your life, I promise you!"

A number 9 streetcar drove past, drenching

them both with puddle-water. "It's too late," said Ostenfeld. "That's the streetcar she said she was going to catch."

"You can still make it!" Hilda hopped from foot to foot. "It has to slow down to pick her up, doesn't it? Run, Mr Ostenfeld!"

Mr Ostenfeld looked at Hilda and a sudden fire ignited in his eyes. He broke into a run and then a sprint.

"Yes, Mr Ostenfeld!" yelled Hilda. "Seize the day!"

The young man legged it through the rain like a man possessed. The streetcar was far ahead but its backlights were still visible.

"Run like the wind!" screamed Hilda. "Don't let her get away!"

The lights of the streetcar stayed still awhile, twinkling in the driving rain, then disappeared into the distance.

"Quite an adventure," said Alfur. "Wait – are you crying?"

"No." Hilda wiped her cheeks. "These are raindrops." She turned abruptly and almost bumped into the group of men standing behind her, all of whom were elderly Ostenfelds.

"Did he make it?" one Ostenfeld asked. "Did he catch the bus in time?"

"We'll never know," said another Ostenfeld.

"I think he caught it," said a third. "I think he caught it – caught it – caught it – caught it–"

Hilda stared at him. "Are you all right?" she asked. "Do you want me to call a doctor?"

"Caught it – caught it – caught it," said Mr Ostenfeld, glitching and flickering like a bad TV signal.

"Oh dear," said Alfur. "I think something rather scary is about to happen."

He was right. A giant shadowy snake emerged from the darkness and rain, slithering fast along the street towards them. Its churning coils shoved a taxi off the road and snapped an ornate iron lamp post clean in two.

"What's going on?" stammered Hilda.

"Let me see now." Alfur paused to choose his words carefully. "You remember how Mr Ostenfeld mentioned the possibility of horrible consequences if you go back in time and change things?"

"Yes."

"Well, voila," said Alfur. "The specific horrible consequence in front of you is what people sometimes call a time worm. Although they tend to pronounce it more like this: TIME WORM!!!"

The monstrous creature lunged towards them. Its bulbous head was pockmarked by three holes: two blank, staring eyes and an O-shaped mouth. The stripes along its body tapered from blue at the head to bright red at the tail. Hilda looked on in horror as the time worm's mouth hole gaped wide open and – chomp! – it devoured one of the Ostenfeld clones in one terrible gulp.

"Quick!" cried Hilda. "Back inside the club!"

Everybody rushed into the jazz club. Unfortunately, that 'everybody' included the time worm, which proceeded to thrash around, destroying everything in its path. Chairs and tables flew through the air. Candelabras fell to the ground. A candle set fire to a sheaf of piano music.

Hilda stamped out the fire with her big red boots, then leaped under a table as the time worm

barrelled past, swallowing up one Ostenfeld after another in its merciless face-hole.

Strange shimmering windows appeared all over the jazz club. From her hiding place under the table, Hilda gazed through the windows and saw the future busily rearranging itself. In one of them, Mr Ostenfeld was dancing the jitterbug with his lady love and there was a diamond ring on her finger.

The last of the elderly Ostenfelds had seen it too. "How about that?" he laughed, wriggling out from underneath the grand piano. "I guess I did catch that bus, after all!" He chuckled fondly, and looked like he was about to say more, but the time worm rudely interrupted him by swallowing him whole.

"Bad time worm!" yelled Hilda, wriggling out from underneath the table.

The time worm reared up and gazed at Hilda, its hollow eyes and mouth lending it an eerie, ghost-like look.

Hilda spread out her arms. "What do you want with me?" she yelled.

"Perhaps it just wants to return your sketchbook," said Alfur.

"Very funny!" muttered Hilda. She rolled to one side as the time worm attacked, narrowly dodging another massive chomp.

She ran out of the club and the time worm slithered after her. Its breath stank of mildew and decay.

As Hilda glanced back over her shoulder, the creature yawned its gaping maw and shot forward to swallow her up.

Fortunately, Alfur's sketchbook joke had given Hilda an idea. She grabbed the Elan magazine from her pocket and closed it with a snap.

VOOP!

Hilda was back in the Trolberg she knew, standing in the middle of a busy road with buses and cars zooming past on either side. They honked their horns and swerved to avoid her as she dashed to the safety of the pavement.

"Let's think about this," said Alfur. "You are standing on a pavement in present-day Trolberg.

Is it fair to say you've left your building now?"

Hilda opened her mouth to suggest another loophole, then stopped and listened. She could hear a faraway rumbling sound, getting louder all the time.

"Hold that thought," said Alfur. "For now, you should probably concentrate on RUNNING AWAY."

With a crunching of concrete and a tearing of soil, the pavement opened up like a giant zip and the time worm tore its way through into the present.

15

David and Frida walked through the marketplace, carrying shopping bags full of Spanish onions and fresh kintoki ginger. Their shift at the Sparrow Scout Soup Stall was starting in fifteen minutes and they wanted to have all the ingredients ready for chopping. But as they passed Madeleine's Baked Goods Stall, they could not help stopping to feast their eyes on her trays of plump cupcakes smothered in delicious bifröst icing.

Someone else was also interested in Madeleine's special bifröst icing. Trevor was standing close to the stall, his finger hovering over the cupcakes as if trying to choose which one to buy. Every time Madeleine turned her back, that mischievous finger swept across the top of a cupcake and up into Trevor's mouth.

"Say something," Frida hissed to David as another dollop of icing disappeared into Trevor's smirking face.

"You say something," hissed David. "I'm staying out of this."

"Hello there," said a familiar voice.

Frida and David looked up at the woman who had greeted them. It was Hilda's mum.

"Hello," smiled Frida. "Is it true about Hilda? Raven Leader told us that she's grounded and that she can't help us with the soup stall tonight."

"That's right," said Hilda's mum. "You know what Hilda's like. She cares so deeply about everyone and everything but then she takes it too far and she ends up doing things that are just plain naughty."

"That's not true!" David blurted out, and then he realised what he'd said and blushed bright

red. "Sorry, Mrs Hilda's Mum, I didn't mean to be rude, but I don't understand. How can it be naughty to care too much?"

"It can't," said Frida.

"Spot on," said a third voice. "It's Hilda's mum who's naughty, and she can't deny it."

They turned and saw Kertasnikir. Some of the other Yule Lads were hovering behind him, carrying two enormous empty sacks. "That's right, you heard me," Kert said. "But don't you worry, it will all be sorted out. We'll just – WOAH! LOOK AT THAT! THE BIG GLOW IS STARTING!"

David and Frida spun round and stared at the Sonstansil tree for several seconds, trying to spot a telltale pinprick of light among its flowers.

"Don't be daft," said Frida, turning back round to glare at Kert. "There's not even a little glow, let alone a big one."

But Kert was not there to be glared at, and nor were the other two Yule Lads. Oddly enough, Hilda's mum and Trevor had also completely disappeared.

16

As the time worm burst up out of the pavement,
Hilda turned and ran. Reality glitched around her,
opening shimmering time holes on either side.

"Jump through a time hole!" shouted Alfur.

Hilda jumped, and – VOOP! – she landed on
her back on a grassy plain in the middle of a field.
A battlefield, to be precise, where two armies,
human and troll, were enthusiastically bashing the
stuffing out of each other.

Above the din of battle rose a nasal, lilting

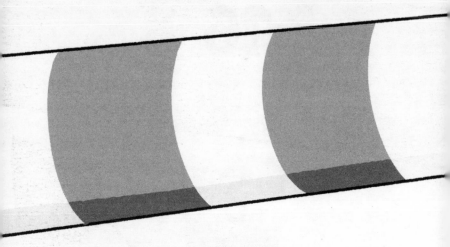

voice. "This is our land now, foul beasts, or my name isn't Edmund Ahlberg!"

Hilda sat up and gawped at her surroundings. Mount Hár and Mount Halldór looked unchanged but the city of Trolberg as she knew it was nowhere to be seen. As Erik Ahlberg's great-great-great-great-great-great-great-great-great-great-grandfather thrust his sword into the air, the time worm burst through the ranks of fighters, sending humans and trolls flying to either side.

"Time hole," said Alfur. "Right above you!"

Hilda staggered to her feet, ran up a troll's back and leaped feet first into the rippling hole.

VOOP!

She landed on a swing in a children's playground. It looked for all the world like Gorrill Gardens, except that the slide and swings were new and brightly painted. A little girl with a dark ponytail sat on the ground nearby, drumming on the grass with a rounders bat.

It's Raven Leader, thought Hilda. I'd recognise those dimples anywhere.

"Look," said the girl. "I'm drumming up worms. They come to the surface because they think it's raining."

A time seam opened up in the middle of the grass and a monstrous worm erupted out of it, thrashing about and dilating its terrible mouth.

"Oooh!" squealed the little girl. "I got a big one!"

Hilda knew that it was herself the time worm wanted to devour, not the little girl. She jumped off the swing, ran up the slide and dived head first into another time hole –

VOOP!

She landed on a dark, deserted street outside her own block of flats. An excited yap from above made her look up. Intelligent black eyes blinked at her from a second-floor window.

"Twig!" cried Hilda. "I'm coming, boy!"

Hilda ran in through the front door and up the stairs towards her flat. As she reached the first-floor landing, Mr Ostenfeld stepped out of his front door into her path.

"Hey!" he cried cheerily. "Come on in and have a piece of cake."

"I can't," panted Hilda. "I'm running away from a time worm."

Mr Ostenfeld smiled sympathetically, then

turned and called into his flat. "Matilda, darling! Hilda and the time worm have arrived."

"Right on time." A white-haired old lady tottered into view, and Hilda recognised her immediately as the young woman from the jazz club, the one Mr Ostenfeld had been dancing with. Deep laughter lines around her eyes and mouth indicated a jolly, well-spent life.

"I don't understand," stammered Hilda. "You're together!"

"We've got you to thank for that," beamed Mr Ostenfeld, putting his arm around his wife's waist. "Forty years of wedded bliss, and all because a blue-haired girl once yelled at me in the rain and told me to run after a streetcar!"

"But, but–" Hilda's mind was whirling. "How did you know about the time worm?"

"Our visitor told us everything," said Matilda, and she stood aside so that Hilda could see into the flat. Sitting on the sofa eating a slice of almond cake was a second Mr Ostenfeld. He smiled and waved at Hilda.

"You weren't the only one to escape from the

jazz club," said the Ostenfeld at the door. "This handsome fellow escaped as well, and he came to warn us about the worm. It's devouring all the irregular timelines, you see."

"I'm so sorry," said Hilda.

"Don't be." Ostenfeld smiled. "Your bravery gave us a lifetime of love, Hilda, and we are deeply grateful to you."

A rumble sounded far away. The building began to vibrate.

"Go inside and cut yourself a slice of almond cake," said Matilda, patting her hand. "You must be hungry after all that running."

"I'm not leaving you," said Hilda. "We'll fight that thing together, all four of us."

"Fight it?" Matilda chuckled. "Why would we want to fight it? A time worm is a very useful monster, when you think about it."

"It's tidying up," Ostenfeld agreed. "Messy business, time travel."

Hilda stared at the couple, who did not seem the slightest bit afraid. Her brain ached from trying to understand what was going on.

"Almond cake," whispered Matilda. "Go on, Hilda, I baked it specially for you. Don't you see, my dear? This is the way it has to be."

As if in a dream, Hilda walked into the flat and sat down next to the unmarried Mr Ostenfeld, who cut a slice of cake and passed it to her. As the front door swung closed, Hilda caught one last glimpse of the married Mr Ostenfeld out on the landing, leaning down to kiss his soulmate. Then the door clicked shut and the rumbling grew to a roar.

Hilda closed her eyes. With trembling fingers, she lifted the cake to her lips.

Chomp.

Hilda opened one eye and looked at the door, fully expecting the time worm to come crashing through at any second.

"Don't worry," said Mr Ostenfeld. "It's gone."

"You mean, it doesn't want to eat me?"

"Not any more," said Mr Ostenfeld. "The timeline has been fixed, you see. You're here. I'm here. I'm not married. Everything is just how it was, except that I'm happier now, and a little less foolish."

Hilda looked at him. "So you're not going to order any more magazines?"

"No, I'm done with that hocus-pocus. Besides, I have something much better to remember her by." Mr Ostenfeld went to a shelf, took down a large photo album and handed it to Hilda.

She turned the pages, marvelling at all the snapshots of Mr and Mrs Ostenfeld's life together. Birthdays. Dinner parties. Holidays. Friends. A happy life, lived to the full.

Hilda managed a small smile. "You called me a meddlesome little rascal," she said.

"Did I?" Mr Ostenfeld chuckled. "Well, I'm very glad you were."

17

Hilda nestled under the blankets with Twig, reading by the light of her bedside lamp. She was on the second-to-last chapter of *Cities and their Unfriendly Occupants* and was appreciating the cosiness of her bedroom like never before. After the trauma of encountering a time worm, being grounded no longer seemed so terrible.

Alfur was reading too. Propped on a pillow beside her, he was halfway through the used copy of Elan magazine that Mr Ostenfeld had given to Hilda as a souvenir. When the old man had

handed her the magazine, he had also pressed a crisp twenty-kronor note into her palm, telling her jokily to "use it as a bookmark".

"Page turn, please!" called Alfur, for the fifty-seventh time.

Hilda reached out and turned the page for her friend, revealing a line drawing of a familiar-looking boy.

"Kertasnikir!" gasped Alfur. "What's he doing in a 1947 copy of Elan magazine?"

Hilda looked at the heading at the top of the page. "Tales of Winter Lore," she read. "Look, Alfur, it's a collection of wintery legends from the olden days."

Halfway down the page was a section heading: GRYLA AND THE THIRTEEN YULE LADS.

"Be good or Gryla will get you!"
Many a misbehaving child has heard this grim warning, but few of them are aware of the legend behind the phrase. Gryla was (and some say, still is) a colossal shaggy-haired ogre. Her main occupation? Catching naughty children and making them into stew!

One year, Gryla caught thirteen naughty boys, the 'Yule Lads' as they are now known.

Their names were:

1. **Kertasnikir**
   (Candy Snatcher)

2. **Hurdaskellir**
   (Door Slammer)

3. **Stekkjastaur**
   (Sheep Botherer)

4. **Giljagaur** (Milk Slurper)

5. **Askasleikir** (Bowl Licker)

6. **Pottasleikir** (Pot Licker)

7. **Stufur**
   (Burnt Pan Licker)

8. **Skyrgamur**
   (Yoghurt Gobbler)

9. **Bjugnakraekir**
   (Sausage Swiper)

10. **Pvorusleikir**
    (Spoon Licker)

11. **Gattapefur**
    (Door Sniffer)

12. **Ketkrokur**
    (Meat Stealer)

13. **Gluggagaegir**
    (Window Peeper)

Gryla intended to make them into stew, but the boys suggested a better course of action. They offered instead to become her servants and kidnap other naughty children for her to eat. From that day on, Kertasnikir and his gang have traipsed the land every winter, snatching naughty children and leaving them in sacks under the Sonstansil tree for Gryla to make into stew. The Yule Lads' farmhouse magically appears in town or countryside, and disappears only when their grisly work is done.

Hilda stopped reading and looked at Alfur in horror. "Kert didn't say anything about feeding anyone to anything."

"He's been lying to you the whole time," said Alfur.

Hilda clapped her hand over her mouth, recalling Kert's excitement at having solved the Trevor riddle. Then she remembered something even worse – Gluggagaegir scribbling Mum's name in his dog-eared notebook.

"Tontu!" yelled Hilda.

Tontu poked his head out of her desk drawer. "Let me guess," he sighed. "You want me to take you somewhere super-fast. Well, I'm sorry, but you can't keep using Nowhere Space for everyday travel."

"EVERYDAY TRAVEL?" Hilda pulled on her sweater and tied her yellow scarf around her neck. "It's not every day your mum faces being KIDNAPPED by a bunch of HOOLIGANS so she can be fed to an OGRE, is it?"

"In your life," Tontu muttered, "that's actually not far from an average day."

Hand in hand they dived behind Hilda's bookshelf, sprinted through Nowhere Space and leaped through a glowing portal that led directly into the Edmund Ahlberg Café. Festival-goers drinking hot chocolate at a low, round table were astonished to see a blue-haired girl, a deer fox and a fuzzy-faced house spirit emerge from under the tablecloth and bolt out into the night.

Hilda, Twig and Tontu sprinted past Madame Lindgren's Gifts, Sandi's Sugar Shack, Torben's Toys and Madeleine's Baked Goods.

Loitering under the Sonstansil tree, stamping their feet and blowing on their hands, were the thirteen Yule Lads.

"Good evening, Kertasnikir," said Hilda loudly. "Or should I call you Candy Snatcher?"

"Kert will do just fine," said Kert. He grinned uneasily and cast a guilty glance at two large burlap sacks under the Sonstansil tree. Some of the boys were throwing handfuls of snow on to the sacks, as if to try and camouflage them.

Hilda's heart sank. Mum and Trevor had already been kidnapped. They were going to be fed to Gryla the ogre – and it was all her fault.

"Mum!" Hilda wailed. "Are you in there?"

"She can't hear you." Kert shuffled his feet in the snow. "They're both perfectly comfortable, though. We gave them something to help them sleep."

"We take no pride in our work," added Gluggagaegir. "But we're bound to it, you see. Cursed by our own naughtiness."

The other Yule Lads stayed silent, hanging their heads in shame.

"Let's get one thing straight," said Hilda, hands on hips. "None of you are naughty. You just did some naughty things – like kidnapping my mum and stuffing her in a sack – but you can make it right again, you really can."

"How?" said Kert. "Gryla will be here soon, and she's expecting a slap-up feast. If we don't have anything for her, she'll be furious."

"You don't want to see her when she's angry," quavered Gluggagaegir, his lower lip trembling.

Tontu tugged on Hilda's sleeve, directing her attention to a massive sign nearby:

"Listen up, Lads," Hilda said. "I think it's time we introduced some variety to your ogre's diet."

David and Frida were busy chopping vegetables when Hilda approached.

"I thought you were grounded," said Frida. She tipped a mound of button mushrooms into the cauldron and made a brief note on her clipboard.

"I am," said Hilda. "But something came up."

"Let me guess," said Frida. "Does it involve some urgent course of action we need to take to avert some horrifying catastrophe?"

"Pretty much," Hilda admitted.

She told them about the Yule Lads and about Gryla's imminent visit. While she talked, David's hands started trembling so much he had to put his knife down.

Frida was excited to hear what Hilda had found out about the Yule Lads, but when she heard Hilda's plan she was reluctant to share her great-great-grandmother's secret recipe with the Yule Lads. "Why can't we just make the soup ourselves?" she asked.

"We could," said Hilda, "but what about next winter, and the winter after that? To keep Gryla happy, the lads must learn how to feed her every year."

"Fine." Frida picked up an onion and chopped it rat-tat-tat into a dozen slices. "Bring those goofballs over here, and I'll give them the best cookery lesson of their lives!"

18

Late that night, Frida, David, Hilda and Twig sat
high in the boughs of the Sonstansil tree. Around
them, clinging to the thick branches, hung seven of
the thirteen Yule Lads: Kertasnikir, Hurdaskellir,
Stekkjastaur, Giljagaur, Askasleikir, Pottasleikir
and Stufur.

"I love it up here," whispered David. "You can
see the whole city, all the way down to the fjord."

As Hilda gazed out across the rooftops and
deserted streets, she noticed a hunchbacked
creature lumbering along Fredrik Road towards
the marketplace. She recognised it as the same
creature she had seen from the airship and from
the Bottle Opener bell tower.

The hump on Gryla's back was overlaid with dirty rags and matted bear skins. Her wrinkly, warty knuckles hung close to the ground, and her body hair was so overgrown that it dragged in the snow in filthy clumps. Most horrifying of all were the clusters of empty wire cages that hung from the leather harness slung across her back – intended, no doubt, for a cargo of naughty boys and girls.

Kert had seen it too. "Everyone be quiet," he whispered. "Here comes our mistress!"

Gryla hobbled into the town square and looked up at the Sonstansil tree. What Hilda had mistaken for a hood was in fact the ogre's hair, which hung down in greasy curtains on either side of her face. And what a face it was, scarred and lopsided, with a long nose and one bloodshot, bulging eye.

Twig shifted on his branch and craned his neck to watch. His tail was now in Hilda's face, tickling her nose. Don't blink, she told herself. And whatever you do, don't sneeze.

Gryla came closer, shambling along with that heavy, lopsided gait of hers. She came to the burlap sacks at the foot of the tree, opened the mouth of the nearest sack and sniffed.

Hilda held her breath. She knew that these sacks under the Sonstansil tree were certifiably one hundred per cent meat-free. Right this minute, Skyrgamur, Bjugnakraekir and Pvorusleikir were carrying a sleeping Trevor back to his bed, and Gattapefur, Ketkrokur and Gluggagaegir were taking Mum to hers.

Gryla scowled. She reached into the sack and removed the topmost carton of Special Sparrow Scouts Soup, her bloodshot eye widening still further in surprise and displeasure.

Hilda watched the ogre prise open the lid, the soup's rich vapours forming a visible wreath around its ugly head. Way up high on her treetop perch, Hilda could smell the buttery aroma of potato, the mellowness of turmeric and the sharp tang of chilli and ginger.

Gryla dipped her finger into the broth and tasted it. On the branch next to Hilda, Frida stiffened. This was the true test of her great-great-grandmother's secret recipe. Could a devourer of children ever be satisfied by a meat-free broth?

The ogre chewed thoughtfully.

She swallowed.

A smile creased the corners of her mouth.

There was a brief commotion in the branches of the Sonstansil tree – a triumphant clenching of fists and a flurry of silent high fiving – but Gryla did not notice. Slowly and carefully she replaced the soup carton in the burlap sack and tightened the drawstring. She grabbed a sack in each hand, set her face towards the mountains and trudged off through the snow, dragging her soup behind her.

As soon as the ogre was out of earshot, the children let out a great sigh of relief.

"She loved it!" cried Kertasnikir. "I've never seen her smile before!"

"So what are you going to do now?" Hilda asked him. "Are you and your brothers going to carry on working as Gryla's servants?"

"Of course," said Kert. "She's a big softie, once you get to know her. Even more so now that she's stopped – you know – eating children."

As the Yule Lads swung their way down

through the Sonstansil tree, a flower by Hilda's left shoulder unfurled its petals silently and began to gleam.

"Look," whispered Frida. "The Big Glow has begun!"

Hilda gazed wide-eyed at the bioluminescent beams that shone from the centre of each bloom, projecting pinpricks of soft light across the city and beyond.

People were already emerging from their houses and gathering in the marketplace. The flowers shone down on the wide-eyed throng, brightening their faces – and their hearts.

"Incredible," murmured Hilda. "I've never seen anything so beautiful in all my life."

A thin ray of flower-light slanted through a gap in the curtains and glimmered on Mum's eyelids. She rubbed her eyes, got out of bed and shuffled to the window to look out.

A patch of lightening sky at the base of Mount Halldór announced the arrival of dawn. Silhouetted against it, Trolberg's skyline stood to attention, a legion of familiar shapes including the jagged contours of the Bottle Opener, the pinnacle of Flimflåm Bank and the bald pate of the raven god poking up above the shops and cafes of Trolberg marketplace.

However, it was the Sonstansil tree that really drew the eye. The top third of the tree was visible from Mum's bedroom window, dotted with pretty, glowing lights. Mum stood and gazed for several minutes, then put her slippers on and hurried out of the room.

"Hilda," Mum whispered, as she padded along the corridor. "The Sonstansil tree is blooming. Come and see!"

She pushed open Hilda's bedroom door and peered inside. Hilda's duvet was rumpled but the bed was empty.

"Darling?" Mum turned and hurried along the corridor, anxiety rising in her chest. It was just like Hilda to sneak out of the flat and go on some terrifying nocturnal adventure, even when she was supposed to be grounded. "If you're not here, there will be no fudge pops for six months!"

A narrow strip of light shone out from under the living-room door. Mum opened the door and there in front of her, sprawled on the sofa, was Hilda. She was upside-down with her head an inch off the floor and her heels hooked over the back of the cushions, reading the very last page of *Cities and their Unfriendly Occupants*. Twig was curled up next to her, snoring softly.

"There you are!" said Mum. "How long have you been up?"

"A while," said Hilda.

"Guess what?" said Mum. "The Sonstansil tree is blooming!"

"Wow!" Hilda did her best to sound surprised. "Can I see?"

They went to the window and stood there side by side, gazing at the majestic, glowing tree.

"I had the most extraordinary dream," said Mum. "I was buying cupcakes at Madeleine's Baked Goods Stall, and the next thing I knew, I was in some sort of sack – " She paused and shook her head. "I need to stop eating cheese at bedtime."

"Mum," said Hilda. "There's something I want to tell you." For a moment, she considered telling her mother the whole story – Yule Lads, time travel, Gryla and all – but then she thought better of it. "I got you a present."

She scooted off and came back holding a carefully wrapped package with a gift tag in the shape of an artist's palette.

"Thank you, Hilda!" Mum took the package and started to unwrap it.

Hilda had spent most of Mr Ostenfeld's twenty-kronor gift on extra vegetables for Gryla's soup, but she had managed to keep back five kronor for the most important purchase of all. On the curve of Mum's palm sat a smooth round snow globe containing a little bludbok tree. It was a perfect miniature, complete with dark hollows, speckled leaves and even a tiny squirrel's nest.

Mum put a hand over her mouth, and she looked as if she was going to cry.

"What's wrong?" said Hilda. "Don't you like it?"

"I love it," croaked Mum. "And I love you too,

Hilda, more than words could ever express."

It had begun to snow outside, and the falling flakes made it seem for all the world as if the lights on the Sonstansil tree were twinkling. Hilda curled an arm around Mum's waist and leaned her head into the softness of her dressing gown.

"Mum," whispered Hilda. "Does this mean I'm no longer grounded?"

Mum chuckled and hugged her tight.

"Good try," she whispered. "Ask me again in a week or two."

How much can you remember from
Hilda and the Time Worm? Answer these
fiendish quiz questions to find out!

1. What does ASPECT stand for?

2. How many Yule Lads are there?

3. How much is the snow globe that Hilda wants to buy?

4. What is the mechanical bell-ringer called?

5. What kind of bird is Cedric?

6. How many bell towers are there in Trolberg?

7. What is Mr Ostenfeld's time travelling magazine called?

8. What kind of cake does Matilda give Hilda?

9. What is the Yule Lad called Kertasnikir also known as?

10. What is the name of Trolberg's famous glowing tree?

Answers: 1. Annual Safety Patrol Essay Contest Trophy 2. Seven, but they claim there are 13 3. Five kronor 4. The Bellboy 3000 5. A pigeon 6. 42 7. Elan magazine 8. Almond cake 9. Candy Snatcher 10. The Sonstansil tree.

COLLECT ALL THE BOOKS
IN THE HILDA SERIES...

FICTION BOOKS
Written by Stephen Davies

Hilda and the Hidden People
Hilda and the Great Parade
Hilda and the Nowhere Space
Hilda and the Time Worm
Hilda and the Ghost Ship
Hilda and the White Woff

GRAPHIC NOVELS
Written and illustrated by Luke Pearson
Hilda and the Troll
Hilda and the Midnight Giant
Hilda and the Bird Parade
Hilda and the Black Hound
Hilda and the Stone Forest
Hilda and the Mountain King

Discover more of Hilda's world at
www.hildabooks.com